Dan and Pip's ship is ideal for you to use together when your child:

- enjoys looking at books with you and will join in to sing rhymes and tell stories

- shows interest in the details of illustrations.

Using *Dan and Pip's ship*

- Read *Dan and Pip's ship* to your child. Take time to enjoy the pictures and especially the large foldout illustration in the middle.

- Point to the words as you read, ask what Dan or Pip is doing, and tell your child what the words say.

- The story is presented again at the end of the book. Read it aloud and explain that these words are telling you the whole story.

- Look at all the pictures again. Can your child remember any of the words and say them with you?

A catalogue record for this book is available
from the British Library

Published by Ladybird Books Ltd Loughborough Leicestershire UK
Ladybird Books Ltd is a subsidiary of the Penguin Group of companies

Dan and Pip's ship

written by
Jillian Harker and Geraldine Taylor

illustrated by Anthony Lewis

Ladybird

Cut and...

ore glue

lick

Stamp and ...

Some m

Some gold

lick

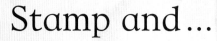

Stamp and...

Some more glue

stick

Some blue

Stitch and...

snip

Dan and Pip's ship

All aboard!

Hoist the sail and…

climb the mast

A sea monster…

swimming past

Wild waves in ...

a stormy sea

A shining ship...

to rescue me!

Dan and Pip's ship

Cut and...
  lick
Stamp and...
  stick

Some more glue
Some gold
Some blue

Stitch and...
  snip

All aboard!

Hoist the sail and...
climb the mast
A sea monster...
swimming past
Wild waves in...
a stormy sea

A shining ship...
to rescue me!

Here are some ideas for things you might do together, using *Dan and Pip's ship* as a basis for other activities.

- **Talk about**
  What kinds of things do children need to make a ship like Dan and Pip's?
  Look back over the pictures to see what Dan and Pip used.
  What would your child call her ship?
  Where would she go in it?
  Has your child ever seen a ship?
  What can she remember about it?

- **Storytelling**
  Use the large foldout picture in the middle of the book to tell your own stories of sea-faring adventures. What might happen on the island? What else might be in the treasure chest?

- **Rhyme and memory**

  How many of Pip and Dan's rhyming activities can your child remember?

  You can cue in one word and your child can tell you its rhyming partner from the story, eg, *Cut and stick, Stamp and...*

- **Reading practice**

  Can your child 'read' the book to you, using the pictures to help her? Pretend – or memory – reading is a vital step on the way to real reading.

Other storybooks in this series:

Peep's asleep

Don't do that, Mop!

You'll lose that bear!